# This book belongs to

_____

# a brilliant brown baby!

This book is dedicated to my father,
Charles A. Williams who always made sure all the brown
babies in his life knew how brilliant they were!

A special thanks to Cortland N. Boone, my very own brilliant brown
baby.

Brilliant Brown Babies
Children's Book Series

Copyright © 2020 Desiree Williams

ISBN-13:978-0578663302

www.brilliantbrownbabies.com

# Brilliant Brown Babies

Written and Illustrated by
Desiree L. Williams

# Brilliant brown babies...

# ...have curly curly hair

# Brilliant brown babies...

# ...always care and share.

# Brilliant brown babies...

...are smart smart smart!

# Brilliant brown babies...

# ...love to make art.

# Brilliant brown babies...

...dance to the beat.

# Brilliant brown babies...

...really move their feet.

# Brilliant brown babies...

...eat yummy yummy food.

# Brilliant brown babies...

# Brilliant brown babies...

...know their history.

# Brilliant brown babies...

# ...roots are rich in victory.

# Brilliant brown babies...

# ...have beautiful skin.

# Brilliant brown babies...

# Brilliant brown babies...

...come from kings and queens.

# Brilliant brown babies...

...are proud of the red, black, and green.

# Brilliant brown babies...

...Have friends that are kind.

# Brilliant brown babies...

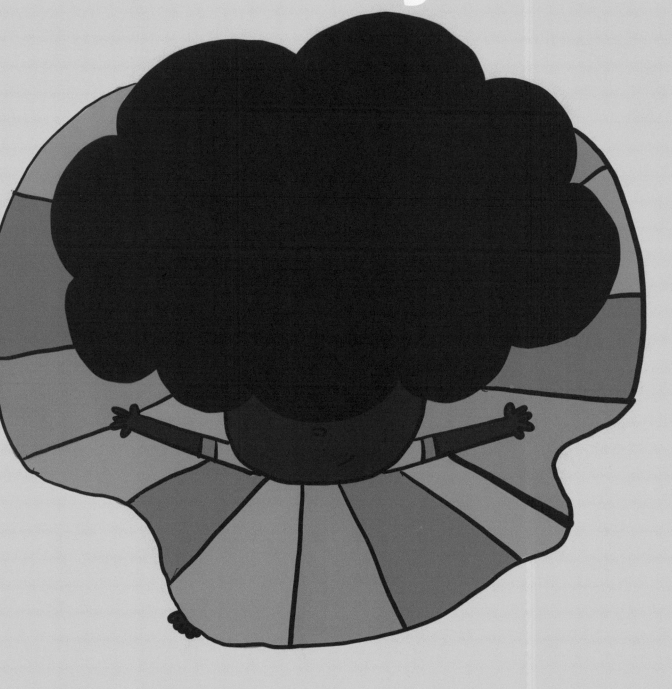